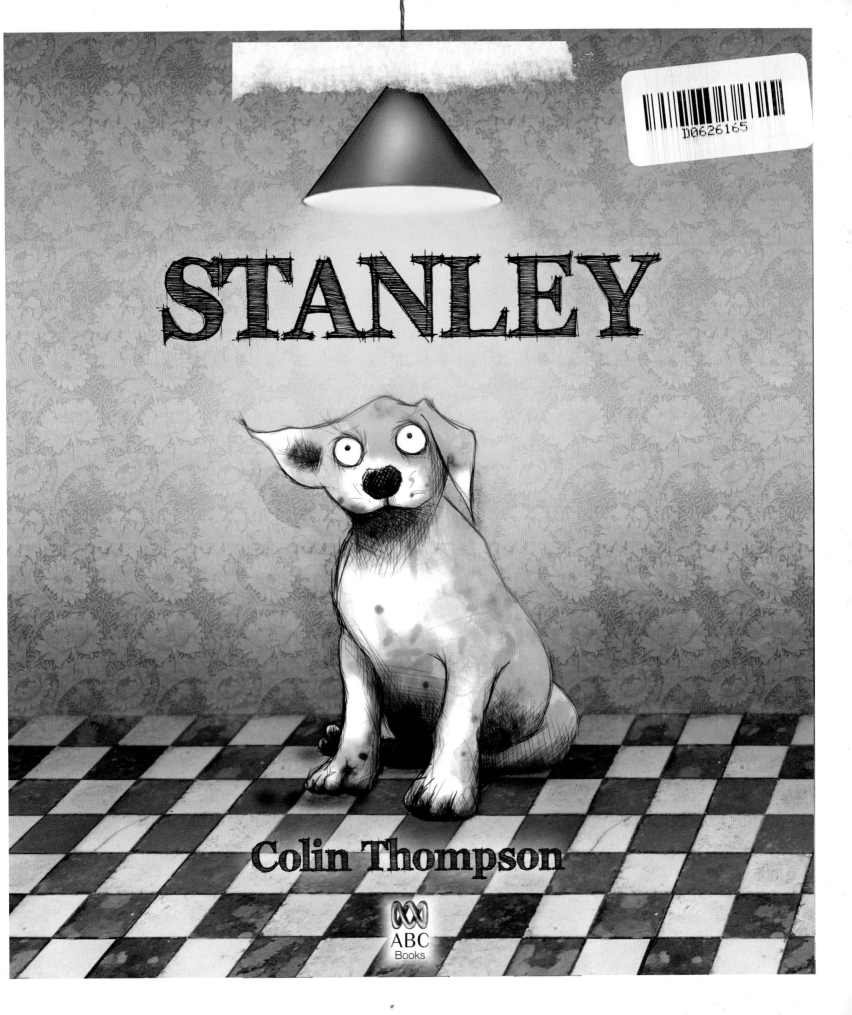

# STANLEY

## Colin Thompson

Stanley looked as if he had been built out of bricks.

Very old bricks that had been around forever, bricks that had been leant against and rained on and loved. Bricks that were as strong as a mountain.

From a distance, Stanley looked dangerous, but if you got up close and looked into his little brown eyes, you could see he was as soft as a pillow.

Stanley loved four things.

He loved his bed, his dinner, his red rubber ball and Gerald, his human.

He also had a blue rubber ball, a garden full of well-chewed bones and Gerald's mum. Stanley liked them a lot, but it wasn't the sort of love that made his tail quiver with happiness like Gerald and his red ball did.

Gerald looked as if he had been made out of paper.

Gently folded and glued together by very careful hands. He looked as harmless as a postage stamp.

If you got up close and looked through his thick glasses into his little blue eyes, you could see that, yes, he was indeed harmless.

Gerald loved three things.

He loved his mum and Stanley and Lego, but not necessarily in that order.

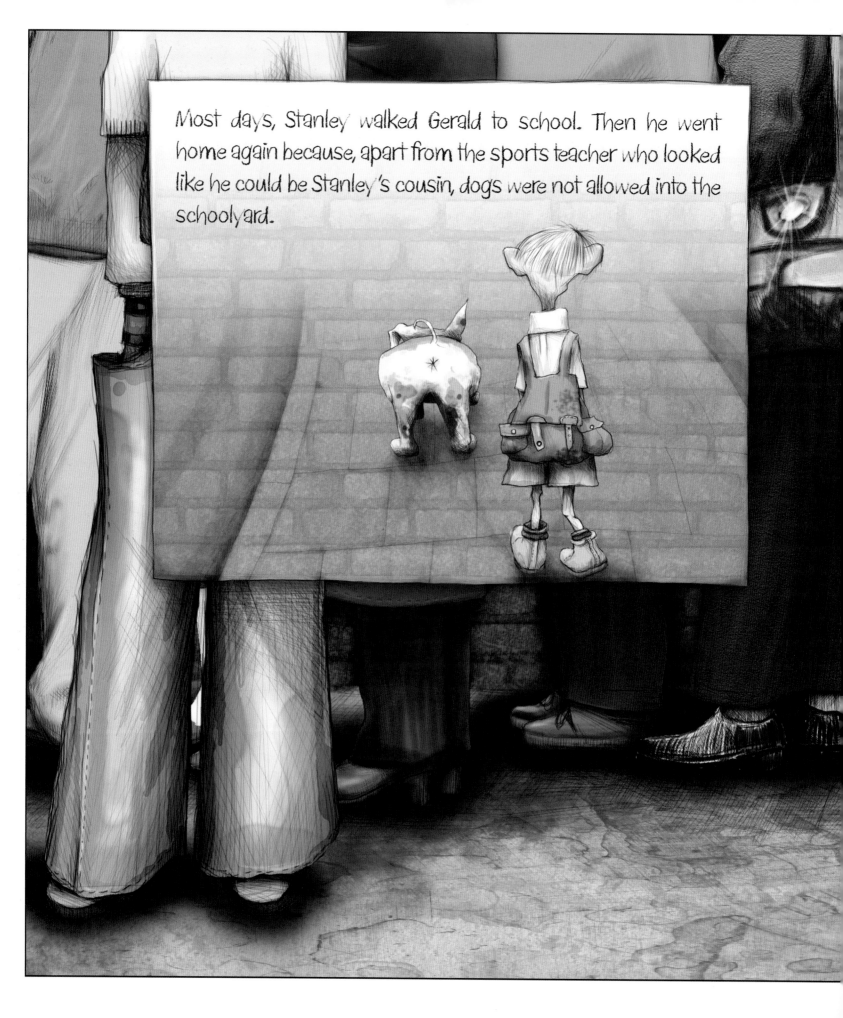

Most days, Stanley walked Gerald to school. Then he went home again because, apart from the sports teacher who looked like he could be Stanley's cousin, dogs were not allowed into the schoolyard.

And when school finished, Stanley went back and waited with all the mums and dads until their children came out. Everyone knew Stanley and, apart from two of those strange sort of people who only like cats, everyone was his friend.

Sometimes Stanley took Gerald's mum to collect him from school, but most days he went on his own. Gerald's dad never went to the school because Gerald didn't have one.

It was very quiet in Stanley's house. There were no brothers or sisters or dads or grannies or other dogs or even a cat, budgie or goldfish. Stanley knew how to bark, but no one had ever heard him do it. There never seemed to be any need to. Nothing bothered him, not even the birds in the back garden when they sat on his head.

\*\*\*\*

Life was peaceful, but sometimes Stanley felt quite lonely. Gerald and his mum were wonderful, but neither of them ever came and curled up in his basket with him. Well, Gerald had when he had been very little, but he hadn't smelt very nice in those days and it had made Stanley's eyes water.

We are, Stanley thought, all alone with ourselves.

The road stopped at the end of Stanley's street and there was a gate in the wall and the gate went into a small park. The park was peaceful too. Sometimes there were other dogs and children and mums and dads and other people like mums and dads who were older and wrinklier.

At home, Stanley's red rubber ball only bounced three times before it hit the fence. In the park, it bounced more times than Stanley could count and his legs got very tired chasing it, but it was so exciting, especially if other dogs chased his ball too.

Most dogs dropped the ball and ran when they saw Stanley charging towards them.

Café · Max

Except for one.

She kept the ball in her mouth and growled.

*That's my ball,* Stanley barked.

The dog barked back but because she had the ball in her mouth, Stanley couldn't understand what she was saying.

Then she ran away.

And took Stanley's wonderful, beautiful red rubber ball with her.

Stanley ran back to Gerald and whinged, but because Stanley was a dog and Gerald was a human, the boy hadn't the faintest idea what he was on about and to make it worse, Gerald didn't even notice Stanley had lost his ball until they got home and his mum said, 'Why didn't you take Stanley's ball with you?'

They went back to the park, but everyone had gone home and there was no sign of the ball.

The next morning, there was a knock at the door.

'My daughter, Felicity, thinks this belongs to you,' said a man, holding Stanley's ball.

'Oh,' said Gerald's mum.

'It's Stanley's,' said Gerald.

*Yes it is, said Stanley, and it's been chewed.*

'Lulu's chewed it a bit,' the man said, 'so we got you another one.'

'You didn't have to do that,' said Gerald's mum.

*Yes, you did, Stanley said to himself. Your dog has completely ruined it. I'll never be able to look at it the same way again.*

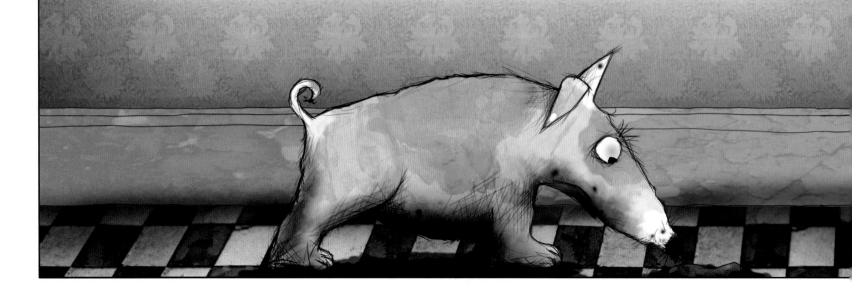

Then the man was in the kitchen and the air was full of coffee and fresh biscuits.

Stanley took his new ball out into the garden and Lulu followed him with the old one in her mouth and they both lay down in the sun.

Nice garden, Lulu said. I'm sorry I took your ball, but I just couldn't help myself.

Love at first sight, was it? said Stanley.

Yes.

I know the feeling.

He had fallen in love with the ball the first time he had seen it and now he had fallen in love all over again with the new one.

Because that's what dogs are like.

Humans don't usually do that.

Not the falling in love bit. They do that, but not with red rubber balls.

In the kitchen with the coffee, Gerald's mum felt a bit strange and that night as she was falling asleep with Stanley snoring quietly on her foot, she realised that the strange feeling was something inside her head that she had forgotten about.

Stanley twitched and did the running in his sleep thing that dogs do and in his sleep he was running round the garden with Lulu.

Humans don't do the running in their sleep thing very often. Gerald's mum was running in her imagination. Well, not so much running as dreaming that maybe, possibly, perhaps she might like to.

The next day, Felicity and her dad came round with Lulu and some more biscuits they'd made.

'Nice garden,' Felicity said to Gerald.

Gerald blushed, mumbled and looked at his shoes.

Felicity, who was almost exactly the same age as Gerald, but without the shy bit, looked at Gerald's shoes and wondered why he was staring at them.

'My dad keeps talking about your mum,' said Felicity, the thirteenth time they visited.

'It's probably her biscuits,' said Gerald, staring at his feet again, but it was ok because he had a new pair of shoes that he hadn't got to know very well yet.

Gerald's mum and Felicity's dad began making biscuits together and calling each other by their first names like they'd known each other for years.

'It's funny,' said Gerald's mum, on the fifteenth visit, 'but it feels like we've known each other for years.'

SUGAR

And they had. They just hadn't met each other until now.

I hope we live in your house, said Lulu. Your garden smells much nicer than mine.

Stanley was too busy to speak. He was trying to wriggle out of the terrible red bridesmaid's dress that Gerald's mum had made out of a tablecloth and squeezed him into that morning.

But it was a small price to pay for having his
house filled up with a whole family.

There is more to life than biscuits and rubber balls, but not much.

The ABC 'Wave' device and the 'ABC KIDS' device are
trademarks of the Australian Broadcasting Corporation and are
used under licence by HarperCollins*Publishers* Australia.

First published in Australia in 2016
This edition published in 2016
by HarperCollins*Children'sBooks*
a division of HarperCollins*Publishers* Australia Pty Limited
ABN 36 009 913 517
harpercollins.com.au

Copyright © Colin Thompson 2016

**HarperCollins*Publishers***
Level 13, 201 Elizabeth Street, Sydney NSW 2000, Australia
Unit D1, 63 Apollo Drive, Rosedale, Auckland 0632, New Zealand
A 53, Sector 57, Noida, UP, India
1 London Bridge Street, London SE1 9GF, United Kingdom
2 Bloor Street East, 20th floor, Toronto, Ontario M4W 1A8, Canada
195 Broadway, New York NY 10007, USA

National Library of Australia Cataloguing-in-Publication entry:

Thompson, Colin, (Colin Edward), author, illustrator.
Stanley / Colin Thompson.
ISBN: 978 0 7333 3286 9 (paperback).
For ages 3–7.
Dogs–Juvenile fiction.
A823.3

Designed and typeset by Colin Thompson
Cover illustrations by Colin Thompson
Colour reproduction by Graphic Print Group, Adelaide
Printed in China by RR Donnelley on 128gsm Matt Art

5 4 3 2   17 18 19

Visit Colin Thompson's website: www.colinthompson.com